this book belongs to Rebecca Thomson

THE TALE OF PETER RABBIT AND BENJAMIN BUNNY

From the authorized animated series
based on the original tales

BY BEATRIX POTTER

F. WARNE & Co

Once upon a time there were four little rabbits, and their names were Flopsy, Mopsy, Cotton-tail and Peter.

They lived with their mother in a sandbank, underneath the root of a very big fir-tree.

'Now, my dears,' said Mrs Rabbit one morning, 'you may go into the fields, or down the lane but *don't* go into Mr McGregor's garden.

'Run along now and don't get into mischief. I am going out.'

Then old Mrs Rabbit took a basket and her umbrella and went through the wood to the baker.

'Now then, a loaf of brown bread and, let me see, five currant buns,' she said.

Flopsy, Mopsy and Cotton-tail, who were good little bunnies, went down the lane to gather blackberries. But Peter, who was very naughty, ran straight away to Mr McGregor's garden. On the way he saw his cousin Benjamin.

'Meet me tomorrow - at the big fir tree!'

Peter squeezed under the gate into Mr McGregor's garden. First he ate some lettuces and some French beans. And then he ate some radishes. 'Ooh! My favourite,' he said happily.

Then, feeling rather sick he went to look for some parsley. But whom do you think he should meet round the end of a cucumber frame?

'Oh help!' gasped Peter.

'It's Mr McGregor!'

Mr McGregor was after him in no time, shouting 'Stop, thief!'

Peter lost his shoes and ran faster on all fours.

Peter might have got away if he had not got caught up in a gooseberry net.

'Hurry, Peter, hurry,' urged some friendly sparrows. 'Mr McGregor's coming! Quick, you *must* keep trying.'

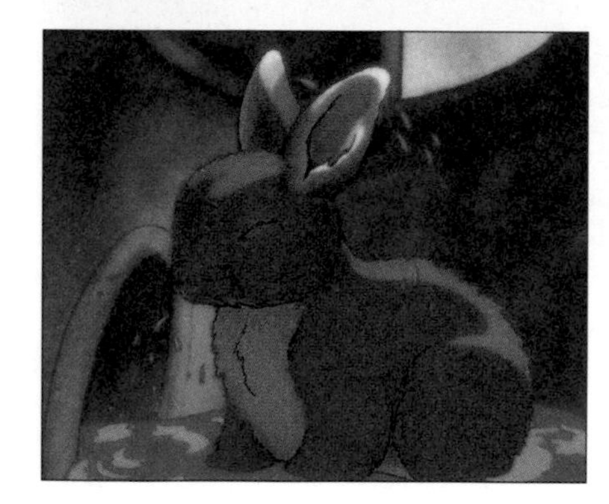

Peter wriggled out just in time. He rushed into the toolshed and jumped into a watering can.

'Come on oot, ye wee beastie – I know you're here somewhere,' muttered Mr McGregor.

Then Peter sneezed, 'Kertyschoo!' and Mr McGregor was after him again.

Peter was quite lost. He saw a little old mouse carrying peas to her family.

'If you please, Ma'am, could you tell me the way to the gate?' he asked.

'Mmmm,' was all she could mumble.

Presently, Peter came to a pond where a white cat was sitting. His cousin Benjamin had warned him about cats!

And then Peter saw the gate. He ran as fast as he could, slipped under the gate, and was safely in the wood.

He ran all the way home.

'Where have you *been*?' asked Peter's mother. 'And where are your clothes? That is the second little jacket and pair of shoes you've lost in a fortnight.'

Then Mrs Rabbit put him to bed and gave him a dose of camomile tea. But Flopsy, Mopsy and Cotton-tail had bread and milk and blackberries for supper.

The next day Benjamin Bunny was sitting on a bank waiting for Peter when he heard the noise of a horse and cart.

'Well, what luck! It's Mr and Mrs McGregor going out! I'd better find Peter right away,' thought Benjamin.

'I say!' exclaimed Benjamin. 'You *do* look poorly. Who has got your clothes?'

Peter told him what had happened the day before.

Benjamin laughed. 'That's what I came tell you. Mr McGregor has gone out in the gig, *and* Mrs McGregor.'

Then they heard Mrs Rabbit calling to Cotton-tail to fetch some more camomile.

'Perhaps a walk might make me feel better,' said Peter.

They looked down into Mr McGregor's garden. Peter's coat and shoes were plainly to be seen upon the scarecrow, topped with an old tam-o-shanter of Mr McGregor's.

'It spoils people's clothes to squeeze under a gate,' said Benjamin.

'The *proper* way to get in, is to climb down a pear tree.'

It had rained during the night. Peter's coat had shrunk and his shoes were full of water.

'Mama will be dreadfully angry,' said Peter.

'We can use the handkerchief now to carry onions as a present for Aunt,' said Benjamin.

'Oh no! Mind out, Benjamin.'
Peter wanted to go home.

'Gracious, what now, Benjamin?' asked Peter.
This is what the little rabbits saw round the corner.

'Quick, under here,' urged Benjamin. 'She's coming towards us.'

The cat sat on the basket for *five* hours.
Mrs Rabbit was anxious.
'Leave it to me, Josephine,' said Benjamin's father. 'I think I know where the young rascals have got to. And if I'm right. . .'

Mr Bouncer had no opinion whatever of cats. He kicked the cat into the greenhouse and locked the door.

'Now then, Benjamin first, I think, then Peter. . . . Off home with you now.'

Then Mr Bouncer took the handkerchief of onions, and marched out of the garden.

When Peter got home, his mother forgave him because she was so glad to see that he had found his shoes and coat.

Cotton-tail and Peter folded up the pocket handkerchief and old Mrs Rabbit strung up the onions and hung them from the kitchen ceiling.

'There now my dears, all's well that ends well. But let that be a lesson to you, Peter.'